THE LITTLE DUTCH BOY

A Tale of Perseverance

Adapted by Sarah Toast

Illustrated by Linda Dockey Graves

PUBLICATIONS INTERNATIONAL, LTD.

Long ago a boy named Hans lived with his mother in a little town in Holland. The land of Holland is very flat, and much of it is below sea level. The farmers there built big walls called dikes to keep the sea from flooding their farms. Hans knew that if a dike broke, the town would be ruined.

One day Hans's mother packed a basket of fruit, bread, and cheese for Hans to take to Mr. Van Notten, their old friend. Mr. Van Notten lived outside of town, and it was a long way to his house. As Hans set out, his mother told him not to stay too late. She wanted him to be home before dark.

To get to Mr. Van Notten's home, Hans just followed the main road out of town. The road ran right alongside the dike.

Hans was very thirsty and hungry after his long walk, so Mr. Van Notten made cocoa and set out the bread and cheese. After their meal, the boy and the old man talked by the fire. Hans enjoyed Mr. Van Notten's stories of the past.

Suddenly, Hans noticed that the sky had become very dark and stormy. He decided that he should leave right away to get home before it started to rain. Hans said good-bye to Mr. Van Notten and promised to come back soon.

Hans walked quickly, but soon the cold, stinging raindrops battered Hans as he struggled against the powerful wind. The weather made it difficult for Hans to walk, but he kept going. "If I just keep putting one foot in front of the other," Hans said to himself, "I'll be home soon."

The strong wind made the trees bend low, and it flattened the flowers. Hans was getting cold, and he had to hold his hat on his head to keep it from blowing away. "I hope my mother isn't upset when I arrive home so cold and wet," he thought.

Hans kept his head down against the wind as he trudged along the road. Hans had no idea he was nearing the town until he lifted his head for a moment. Hans was happy to see the dike right in front of him. He would soon be home and out of the rain.

Suddenly, Hans noticed some water where it did not belong. There was a small hole in the dike, and a trickle of water was seeping through.

Hans knew right away what must have happened. The storm had whipped up the waves of the sea, and the great weight of the pounding water cracked the dike.

"I've got to warn everyone that the dike has sprung a leak!" thought Hans.

Hans ran into town. "Help! We've got to fix the dike!" he shouted.

But no one heard Hans. Everyone was inside, and all the houses had been closed up because of the storm.

Hans knew his mother must be worrying about him, but he also knew that the hole in the dike was getting bigger every minute. If the hole got big enough, the sea would surely push its way through and break the dike. If the dike broke, all would be lost. The sea would flood the farms and wash away the pretty little town.

As fast as he could, Hans ran back to the place where he had seen the water seeping through the dike. He balled up his fist and pushed it into the hole to stop the little stream of water.

Hans was proud that one small boy could hold back the sea. He was sure that his worried mother would send people to look for him. But minutes turned into hours as Hans patiently stood there.

As darkness fell, Hans became very cold and tired, and his arm began to ache. He had to force himself to keep standing on his tired legs.

As Hans stood in the cold rain by the dike, he thought about the warmth of the fireplace at home. This thought helped the exhausted boy get through the long night.

When Hans didn't come home that evening, his mother began to worry. Then she decided that Hans must be at Mr. Van Notten's house, waiting for the storm to end.

After looking out the door one more time, Hans's mother closed up the house and went to bed, but she couldn't sleep. She was too worried about her little boy.

Early the next morning, Mr. Van Notten was walking to Hans's house. When he came to the dike, he found Hans trembling with cold. Hans's arm hurt from plugging up the dike, and his legs were ready to collapse from standing all night. Still Hans had to hold firm while Mr. Van Notten ran into town to get help.

"Don't worry, Hans," said Mr. Van Notten. "I'll be back in a jiffy. You're doing a great job, just hang on a little longer." Soon Mr. Van Notten returned with someone to take care of Hans and materials to repair the dike.

Word quickly spread through the town of how Hans had held back the sea all by himself. The townspeople went to see the hole in the dike that Hans had kept plugged. Everyone in town thanked Hans for holding back the mighty sea and for saving them from a terrible flood.

The mayor of the town presented Hans with a medal to honor his bravery and dedication, and all the townspeople cheered loudly. Hans would forever after be remembered as a hero. Years later, after Hans was grown up, people still called him the little boy with the big heart.

One to Grow On
Perseverance

When Hans discovered a leak in the dike, he knew he had to stop it. Because he couldn't find help, he plugged up the leak himself and stood his ground for hours. Even though it was dark and cold in the storm, Hans knew that he was the only person who could keep the town from being washed away. That kind of dedication is called perseverance.

Perseverance means sticking with something even when it gets difficult. It helps us through hard times and leads us to great accomplishments.